Princess Beatrice
and the Rotten Robber

For Josephine

Princess Beatrice
and the Rotten Robber

Elizabeth Honey

ALLEN & UNWIN

Once upon a time there was a princess called Beatrice,
who lived in a huge castle in a faraway kingdom.

Princess Beatrice loved dressing up,
and more than anything else she loved
wearing jewels, *lots* of jewels.

Now, in the castle there were rooms and rooms
full of jewels, and her mother and father said
she could wear anything she wanted.

One morning a daring robber
was galloping past the castle,
looking for treasure.
He spied the open door.

'*Yahoo!*' he whooped,
and charged right in.

Turning a corner he ran slap bang into Princess Beatrice.
He couldn't believe his eyes!
At first he thought she was some sort of Christmas tree.
'BONANZA!' he crowed. 'Just look at those glittering goodies!'

'No time to waste!' he cried.
'I'm taking these jewels, Princess and all!'
And with that he swept her up
and dashed for the castle gate.

Now, the horse didn't like the jingle jangle of the jewels.
He snorted and bucked, and with a wild toss of his head
he bolted over the castle drawbridge
and away into the forest.

At breakneck speed they galloped
deeper and deeper into the woods,
bumping and bouncing, twisting and turning.

Jewels flew off like sparks,
but Princess Beatrice was too busy hanging on to notice.

At last they arrived
at the robber's dark and tumbledown shack.
'Ha, ha!' said the robber, chuckling with glee.
'Now to get my hands on this lovely loot!'
And with his big clumsy fingers he tried to take off a bracelet.

'*That's* not how you do it!' snapped Princess Beatrice.
'Let *me* show you.'

In a flash she twisted the bracelet around the robber's wrists.
'See! *That's* what you do!'

'And *this* clip goes here!
And that buckle goes *there*!'

'And this goes like this, and that goes like *that*,
and these go *here*, and those go *there*…'

And before you could say ten tiaras,
he was trussed up like a turkey in the royal jewels.

'There!' said Princess Beatrice. 'They really suit you like *that*!'

'Now,' she fumed, 'how am I *ever* going to get home?'

Then she noticed, a little way off, an earring caught on a twig. Further on a ruby glinted, a diamond winked…

'I know!' she cried.
Quickly she hauled the robber onto the horse's back with a rope of pearls, and set off to find her way home, step by step, jewel by jewel.

Back at the castle, the King and Queen were very worried.
The guards had searched the castle from top to bottom four times.
It was dinnertime and her chair was empty.
They knew it was serious.

Then, by the last rays of the setting sun,
they saw something glinting in the distance.

'It's Princess Beatrice!' they cried.
Cheering with joy, they ran to meet her.

'My little treasure!' said the King.
'My precious flower!' said the Queen,
and they both tried to hug her at once.

As for the robber, he was taken to the royal treasury
and given an enormous tin of polish.
'Since you're so fond of gold and jewels,' said the King,
'I'll make you head cleaner and polisher
of the royal treasures. It's a lifetime appointment,
but you *might* get time off for good behaviour.'

Then, feeling very happy, the family sat down to a late dinner.
They had Turkey à la King and Duchess Potatoes,
followed by Queen Pudding with delicious fresh strawberries.
And between mouthfuls, Princess Beatrice told them
all about how she tricked the rotten robber.

'You caught him well and truly!' laughed the King.

'Yes,' said Princess Beatrice.
'And tomorrow I'm going to help him polish!'